rubbadubbers™

Fun in the Tub

Ready-to-Read

Simon Spotlight

New York   London   Toronto   Sydney

Based on the television series *Rubbadubbers*™ created by HIT Entertainment PLC
as seen on Nick Jr.®

by J-P Chanda
photos by HOT Animation

 SIMON SPOTLIGHT
An imprint of Simon & Schuster Children's Publishing Division
1230 Avenue of the Americas, New York, New York 10020

Library of Congress Cataloging-in-Publication Data
Chanda, J-P.
Fun in the tub / by J-P Chanda.— 1st ed. p. cm. — (Ready-to-read)
"Based on the television series Rubbadubbers as seen on Nick Jr."—T.p. verso.
Summary: The Rubbadubbers describe some of the things that make bathtime fun.
ISBN 0-689-86882-0
(1. Baths—Fiction. 2. Stories in rhyme.) I. Rubbadubbers (Television program) II. Title. III. Series.
PZ8.3.I55 Fu 2004
(E)—dc22
2003018653

What shall we do today?

I say we play all day!

We can run!

We can slide!

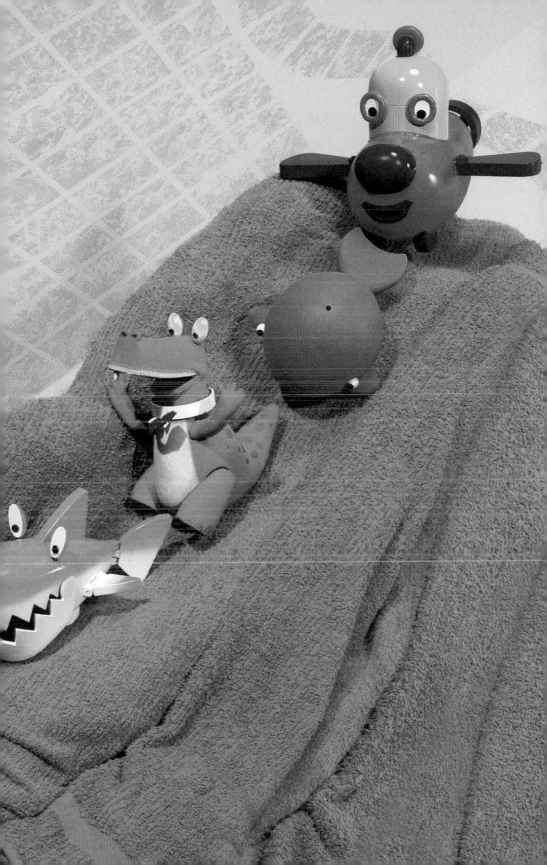

We can skate!

We can hide!

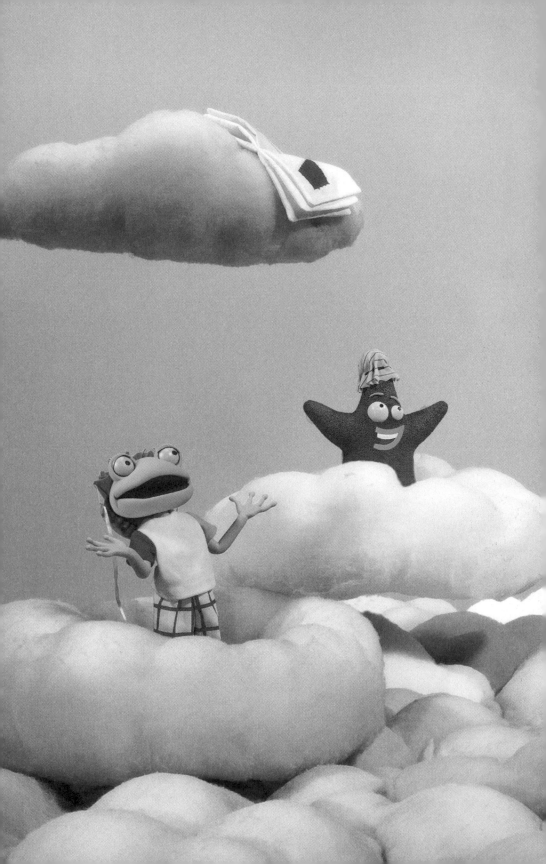

We can zoom!

We can swing!

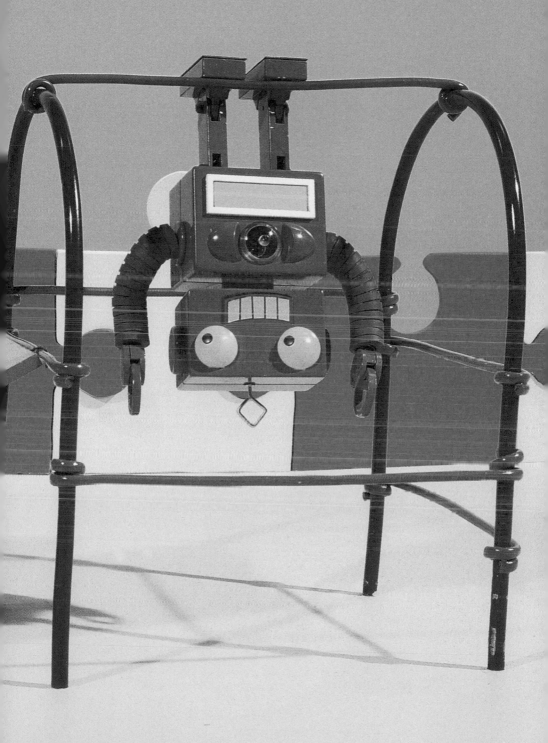

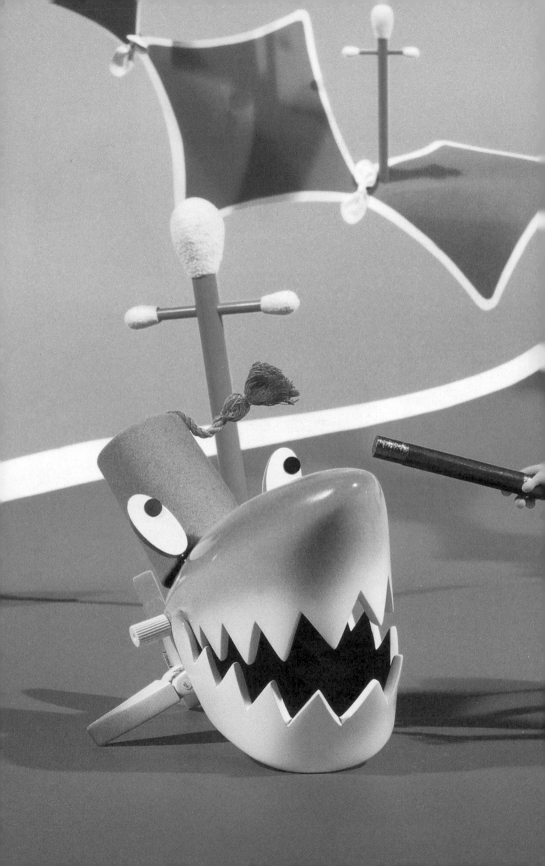

We can dance!

We can sing!

And when the day
is all done . . .

... we can have more bathtime fun!